This book belongs to

....

This edition published by Parragon Books Ltd in 2014
Parragon Books Ltd
Chartist House
15-17 Trim Street
Bath BA1 1HA, UK
www.parragon.com

Written by Steve Smallman
Illustrated by Nicola Slater
Edited by Laura Baker
Designed by Ailsa Cullen
Production by Marina Blackburn

ISBN 978-1-4723-5092-3

Printed in China

PARROTS

GIBBONS

SPOT
A
LOT

AND COUNT
A LITTLE TOO!

ANIMAL
ESCAPE

GIRAFFE

STEVE SMALLMAN   NICOLA SLATER

WARTHOGS

FLAMINGOS

PaRragon

Bath · New York · Cologne · Melbourne · Delhi
Hong Kong · Shenzhen · Singapore · Amsterdam

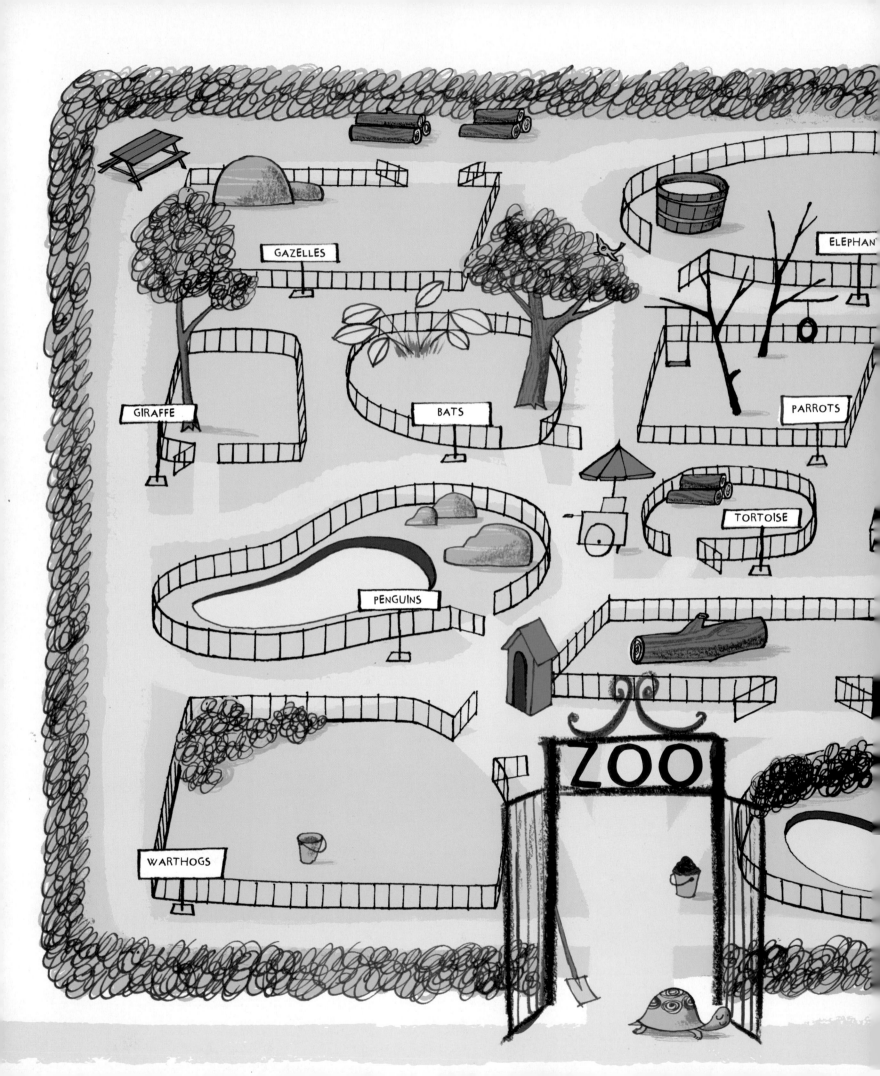

There's trouble at the zoo today...

The animals have run away!

Find and follow the tortoise on every page!

GIBBONS

ZEBRAS

FLAMINGOS

TOWN

ZOO

1 very tall giraffe

Spot the little white mouse.

trying hard not to laugh.

Where is the ladybird?

Find 1 green bird.

2 elephants in socks

playing
peek-a-boo
in the
rocks.

Where is the hippo hiding?

Peek-a-boo!

Spot 3 green lizards.

3 orange gazelles jumping high –

Find my 4 froggy friends.

they don't need trampolines to fly!

Spot 2 penguins doing backflips.

Spot the soaring dog — and his hat!

4 gibbons, long and slim,

Where is my second banana?

Who woke me up?

swinging by the jungle gym!

Spot the balancing lizard.

Who's in there?

Find the jumping mouse.

5 pretty pink flamingos

Spot the pink umbrella.

posing in the cake shop windows!

Find 4 slithering snakes.

6 zebras, white and black,

Spot the dog in a white hat.

crossing over the
road and back.

Spot 4 mice out and about.

Where's my other shoe?

7 batty little bats
wearing silly party hats.

Find a boot out of place.

Spot 10 pink birds
at the party.

Where is the little bumblebee?

8 penguins keeping cool

Where is my pink ball?

splashing at the swimming pool.

Spot 2 bunnies in swimming caps.

9 sneaky little parrots
hiding by the piles of carrots.

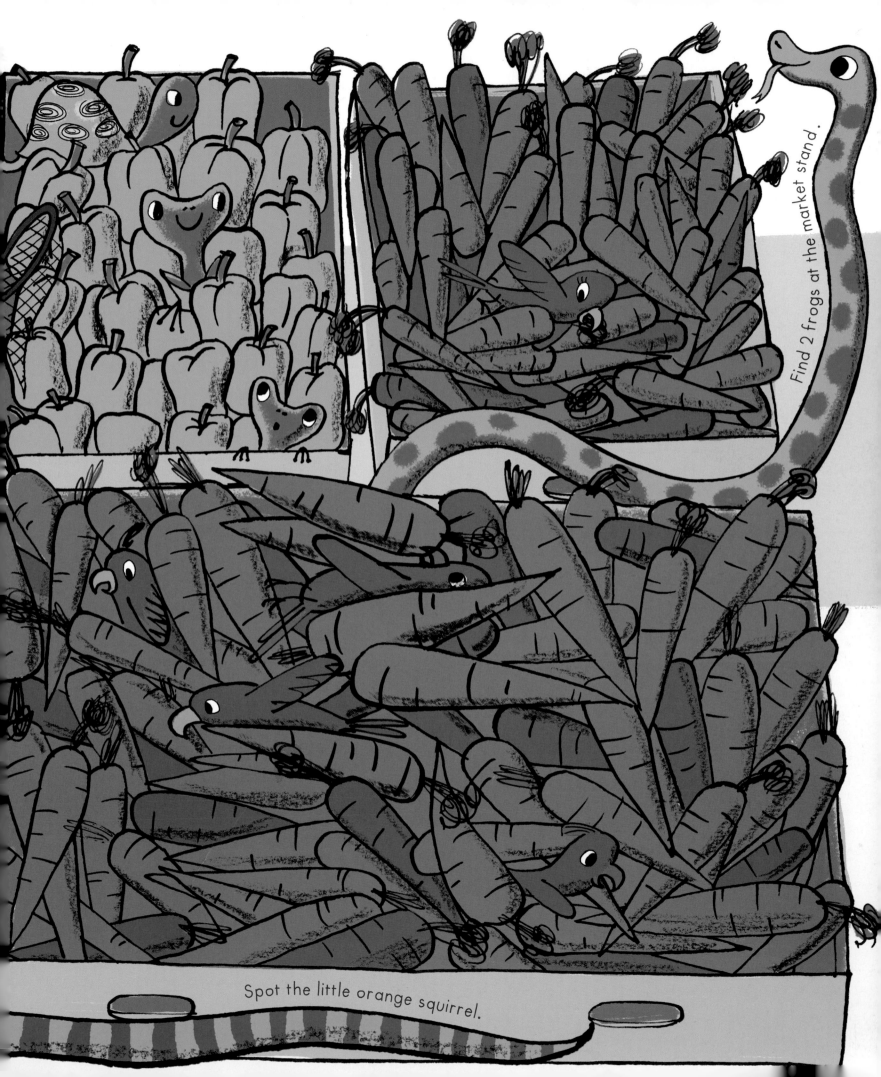

Find 2 frogs at the market stand.

Spot the little orange squirrel.

10 warthogs tapping feet

Spot the snoozing mouse.

Can you find my
2 bunny friends?

dancing to a hip-hop beat!

Where is my orange bag?

Find the fox in sunglasses.

The keeper says,

"Let's have no fuss.
Now, everybody,
on the bus!"

Soon they're back
home in the zoo,

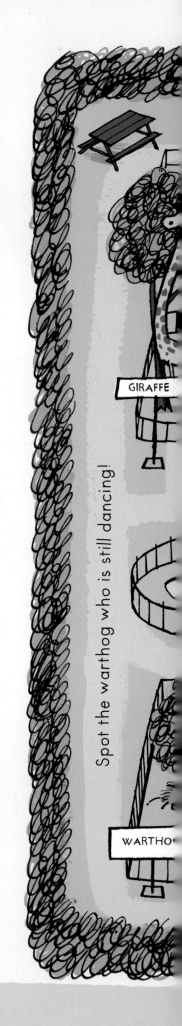

Spot the warthog who is still dancing!

GIRAFFE

WARTHO

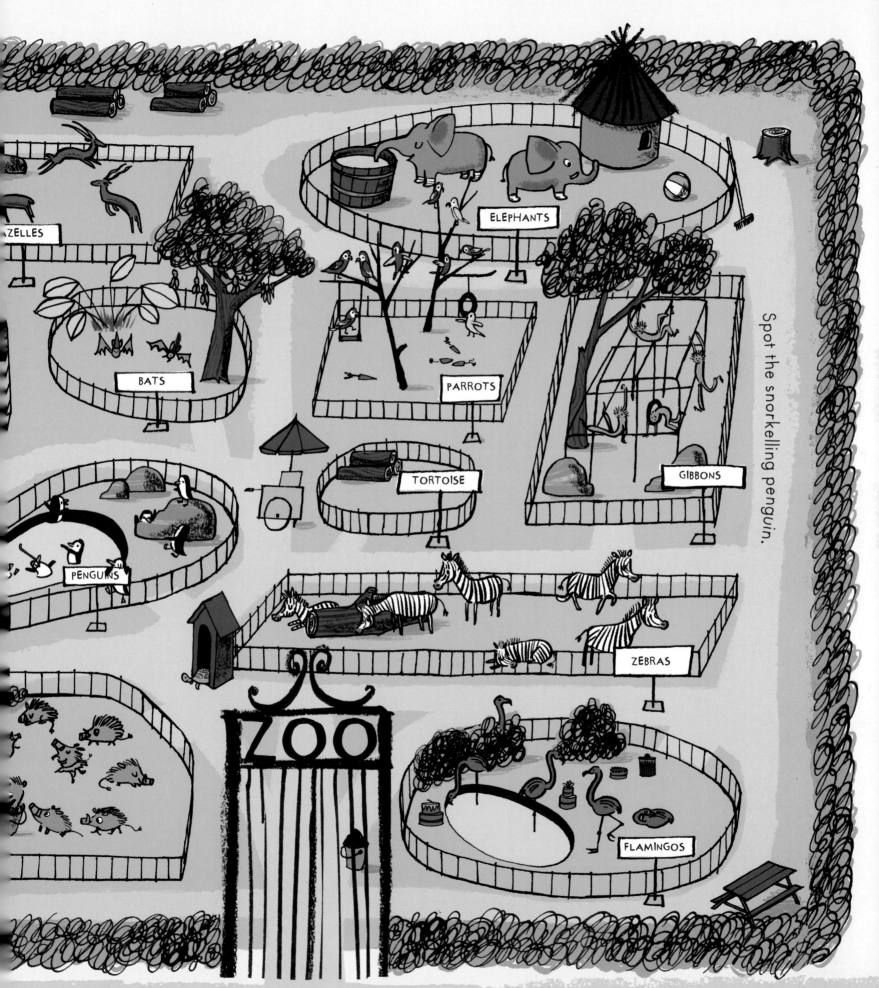

Spot the snorkelling penguin.

but uh oh, Tortoise, where are you?

THE END